Forest of Dreams

Published by
Dial Books for Young Readers
A Division of Penguin Books USA Inc.
375 Hudson Street · New York, New York 10014

Text copyright © 1988 by Rosemary Wells
Pictures copyright © 1988 by Susan Jeffers
All rights reserved
Library of Congress Catalog Card Number: 88-3826
Printed in Hong Kong by
South China Printing Company (1988) Limited
First Pied Piper Printing 1992
ISBN 0-14-054855-6
5 7 9 10 8 6

A Pied Piper book is a registered trademark of
Dial Books for Young Readers,
a division of Penguin Books USA Inc.,
® TM 1,163,686 and ® TM 1,054,312.

FOREST OF DREAMS
is also published in a hardcover edition by
Dial Books for Young Readers.

The art for each picture consists of an oil painting,
which is color-separated and reproduced in full-color.

Rosemary Wells

Forest of Dreams

paintings by Susan Jeffers

A Puffin Pied Piper

God made me new
Just like the spring that waits beneath the snow.

God made me small
Just like the fawn that sleeps inside the doe.

God gave me eyes
To see the woods and all who live within it.
To watch the winter sun last
Every evening one more minute.

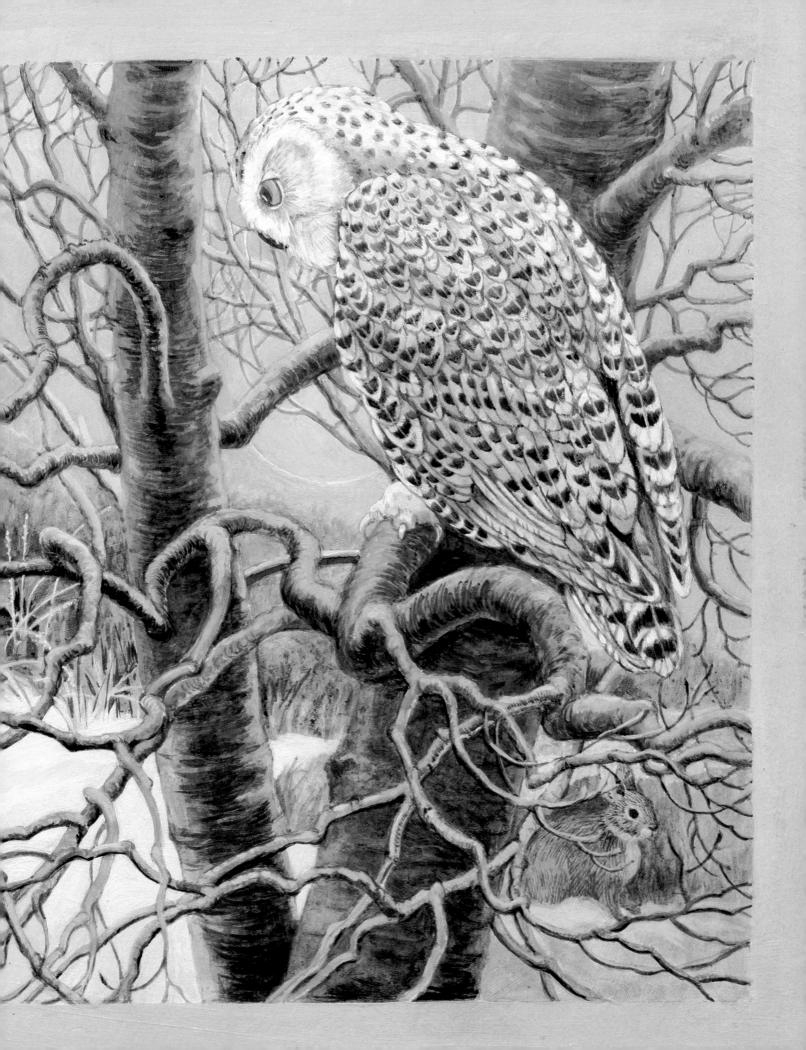

God gave me hands to touch the ice
Stiff and diamond bright,
That spills upon the pine tree
And sparkles up the night.

God gave me strength to climb the tree
Prickly, thick, and high.
I sit inside the winter wind
While all the branches sigh.

Below the frozen salt marsh
There's music in the stream.
God gave me ears to hear it whisper
Like a summer's dream.

God lets me feel
The morning rain, sifting, drifting down.
And I can smell the sunlight burrow
Softly underground.

The earth begins to open
A sparrow starts to sing,

God gave me time to listen.
God gave me everything.

Rosemary Wells

is the author and/or illustrator of over thirty-five books published by Dial. Her picture books include *Max's Chocolate Chicken; Benjamin and Tulip; Noisy Nora;* and *Max's Christmas;* all ALA Notable Books. *Hazel's Amazing Mother,* was a *New York Times* Best Illustrated Book and *The Little Lame Prince* was a *Bulletin of the Center for Children's Books* Blue Ribbon award winner. Her eight pioneering Very First Books about Max and Ruby were praised in *School Library Journal* as "a four-star performance... bound to be early childhood favorites." Her most recent books for Dial include *Max's Dragon Shirt* and *Fritz and the Mess Fairy.*

Susan Jeffers

is internationally acclaimed for her exquisite paintings, and the illustrator of numerous books for Dial—all of which brilliantly portray nature. *Hiawatha* was praised by *School Library Journal,* in a starred review, as a "beautiful artistic experience," and *The Midnight Farm,* written by Reeve Lindbergh, was described by *Publishers Weekly* as a "celebration of life, hope, and wonder." Her most recent books for Dial include *Brother Eagle, Sister Sky: A Message from Chief Seattle,* and *Benjamin's Barn,* also written by Reeve Lindbergh, which was cited by *Booklist* as having "superbly drawn animals" and was one of *Redbook's* Ten Best Picturebooks.

Rosemary Wells and Susan Jeffers have been close friends since the 1960s, when they shared a design studio. Ms. Wells's daughter Beezoo and Ms. Jeffers's daughter Ali served as Ms. Jeffers's models for *Forest of Dreams.*